Wally Saves the Day

Written and illustrated by Catherine Davis

In a magical forest far away, in the hills of Manchester, lived a panda family. The other animals are active in their daily lives, but not Wally.

Wally is a snow-white panda who has no friends. He is tall, with fluffy cheeks, red eyes, and a pink nose. No one knows what his smile looks like, not even his parents, Marvin and May. He often does everything by himself.

One day, Wally decided to walk to the Lucky stream. On his way, he began observing nature when suddenly he saw the most beautiful rose. "What a beautiful rose," he thought as he sniffed the aroma coming from the plant.

It was a Pink rose with red stripes on the edge of the petals.

As he continued towards the stream, he saw Kev the snake slithering by him "Why are you on this side?" Kev scowled at Wally, who was about to walk by Mully the Mulberry bush.

Kev is an average-sized yellow and gold rattlesnake, who was known for stealing. He stopped for a second staring at Wally, who wandered behind the short talking Mulberry bush.

"Hi Wally!" said Mully,"taking your daily walk to the stream I see," the bush continued as Wally nodded and walked by.

"What a weird creature," Kev thought. As he continued his journey towards his home beyond the rocks.

Then suddenly, Wally heard a loud cried. "Kev!" Daisy the Dove scream. "You have done it again, you slithered by and stole my egg," she cried. "My last egg, you have stolen them all," she

continued.

"I did no such thing, Daisy! I was standing near your tree, but only to watch Wally walk by," explained Kev."I haven't been on your branch in weeks".

"Mully, please tell Daisy I did not slither up her branch," Kev cried.   Wally was standing at the stream when he heard a loud fuss. He decided to walk back to the Mulberry to hear what the fuss was about.

"Wally! Did I slither up Daisy's tree while you walked by?" Kev asked. "No you didn't," Wally replied quickly in a grumpy tone. "He was just standing under the tree making fun of me as I walked by Mully," Wally explained to Daisy.

Wally ears started to grow. There was a soft cry, a young dove, but only Wally could hear it. He stopped for a moment. "Shhhhhhh!" He said.

"Did you hear that?"

"Hear what?” asked Kev. “It was the sound of a baby bird,” Wally replied.

“I have no time for your weird nonsense Wally, I cannot find my egg and all feathers are pointing to this sly snake!” Daisy yelled.

“Will you be quiet? There it goes again,” Wally whispered.

Wally stepped behind Mully, and over to the fence that separated the Grassy Meadow from the Magical Forest. The sound of the baby bird got louder and louder.   Wally's ears grew bigger.

On the spur of the moment, Wally saw Sally the snail moving slowly towards an object near her rock.

Wally ran to the baby bird and picked it up. "Daisy! Daisy! I think I have found your baby!" Wally yelled, as he ran towards Daisy and Kev who were still arguing.

"Daisy, your baby!" Wally yelled, as Daisy flew up to peck at Kev's eye.

"My baby!" she yelled, after she flew up the second time, she saw Wally holding the baby dove.

"The egg must have hatched when you went out seeking food, and fell from the nest," said Wally.

"Kev is innocent this time!" Mully shouted!

"Thank you Wally, thank you so much, you saved my life!" Cried Kev. "Thank you Wally, for finding my baby," said Daisy happily.

Wally was seen as a hero from that day on. All the animals became friends and they lived happily ever after.

The End

Let's be creative

Use your imagination to colour the characters.

About the Author

Catherine Davis is a Jamaican educator with over 4 years of local and international teaching experience combined. She uses stories to engage her students from time to time. As a Literacy Specialist and a lover of reading and writing, she decided to make a bold move to publish her own Children's Literature book.